This Walker book belongs to:

_____

_____

_____

for **Nelson**
(good boy)

First published in Great Britain 2008 by Walker Books Ltd
87 Vauxhall Walk, London SE11 5HJ

First published in the United States by Hyperion Books for Children.
British Publication Rights arranged with Sheldon Fogelman Agency, Inc.

20 19 18 17 16 15 14 13 12

This book has been handlettered by Mo Willems.

Printed in China

British Library Cataloguing in Publication Data is available.

ISBN 978-1-4063-1550-9

www.walker.co.uk
www.pigeonpresents.com

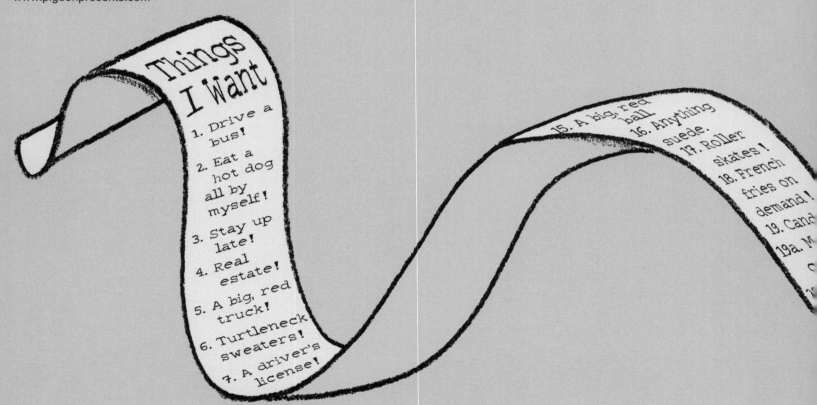

Things I Want

1. Drive a bus!
2. Eat a hot dog all by myself!
3. Stay up late!
4. Real estate!
5. A big, red truck!
6. Turtleneck sweaters!
7. A driver's license!

15. A big, red ball
16. Anything suede.
17. Roller skates!
18. French fries on demand!
19. Cand
19a. M

# The Pigeon Wants a Puppy!

words and pictures by mo willems

WALKER BOOKS
AND SUBSIDIARIES
LONDON · BOSTON · SYDNEY · AUCKLAND

# I WANT
# A PUPPY!
# RIGHT HERE!
# RIGHT NOW!

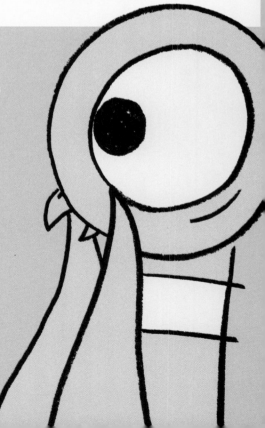

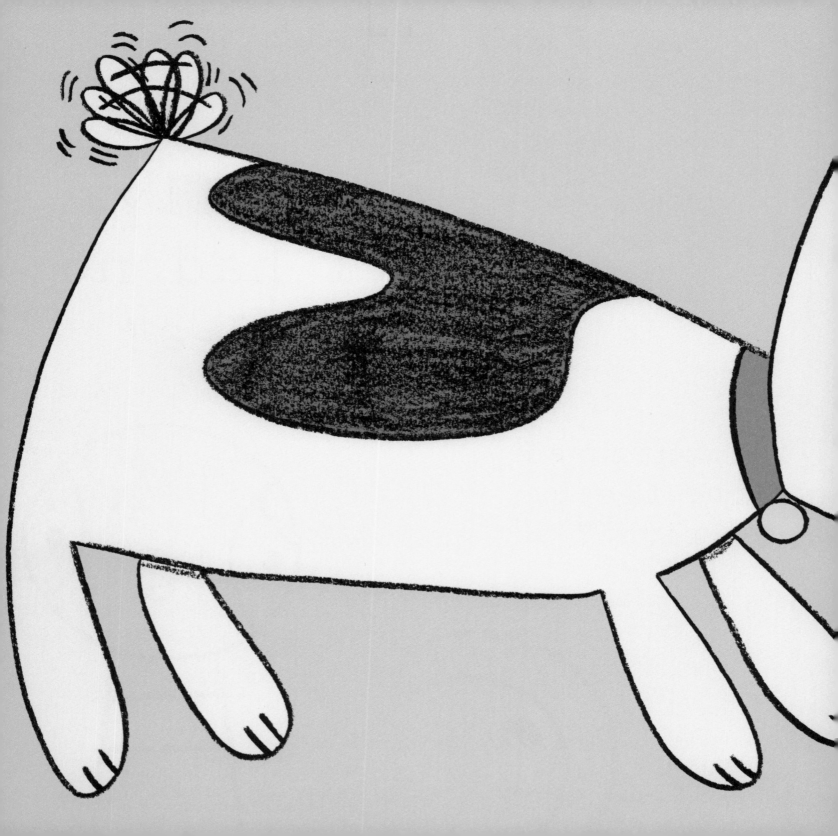